What I Like !

POEMS for the VERY YOUNG

Gervase PHINN

illustrated by Jane Eccles

Published by Child's Play (International) Ltd

Swindon   Auburn ME   Sydney

Text © 2005 G. Phinn   Illustrations © 2005 Child's Play (International) Ltd   All rights reserved

ISBN 1-904550-12-6   www.childs-play.com   Printed in Croatia

1 3 5 7 9 10 8 6 4 2

What I like!

I like spaghetti,
I like cheese,
I like pizza with mushy peas!
Spaghetti and cheese and pizza and peas,
That is what I like -

YEA!

I like fried eggs,
I like greens,
I like juicy tangerines!
Eggs and greens and tangerines,
That is what I like -

YEA!

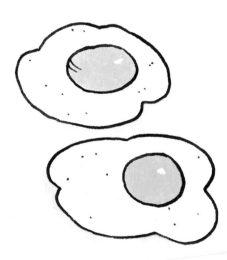

I like burgers
I like chips,
I like ice cream and chocolate whips!
Burgers and chips and chocolate whips,
That is what I like -

YEA!

I like custard,
I like toast,
I like Yorkshire pudding and the Sunday roast!
Custard and toast, Yorkshire pudding and roast,
That is what I like -

YEA!

I love Mum,
And she loves me,
I love all my family!
Mum and me and my family,
That is who I love -

YEA!

Who's a Clever Boy?

I can do my buttons up,
And I can tie my laces,
I can put my underpants on,
And I'm good at pulling faces!

The Lucky Four-leaf Clover

As Dad was bending in a field,
To pick a four-leaf clover,
A billy goat, it butted him,
And knocked poor Father over.

He ran towards a five-bar gate,
And quickly clambered over,
And then fell flat upon his face,
Clutching the four-leaf clover!

Ha! Ha! Ha! and a Hee! Hee! Hee!

Ha! Ha! Ha! and a Hee! Hee! Hee!
I can climb to the top of the tall, tall tree.
Boo, hoo, hoo! Oh dear, dear me!
I've fallen off and cut my knee.

I Like to Fly my Aeroplane

I like to fly my aeroplane,
my aeroplane,
my aeroplane;
I like to fly my aeroplane,
Up in the sky so high!

I like to drive my big black car,
my big black car,
my big black car;
I like to drive my big black car,
Along the open road!

I like to ride my brand new bike,
my brand new bike,
my brand new bike;
I like to ride my brand new bike,
Up and down the hill!

I like to row my small red boat,
my small red boat,
my small red boat;
I like to row my small red boat,
Out on the bright blue sea!

Noises off

The City's full of **Noises**

Cars are honking,
Vans grumbling,
Lorries juddering,
Buses rumbling,
Trams are sliding,
Trains clattering,
Motorbikes spluttering,
Shoppers chattering.

The Forest's full of **Noises**

Rabbits are rustling,
Badgers burrowing,
Slow worms slithering,
Dormice scurrying,
Foxes barking,
Bats squeaking,
Hedgehogs snuffling,
Owls screeching.

The Churchyard's full of **Noises**

Grass is whispering,
Branches creaking,
Blossoms fluttering,
Gate squeaking,
Bushes rustling,
Birds singing,
Bees buzzing,
Bells ringing.

The Beach is full of *Noises*

Gannets are calling,
Sea crashing,
Crabs scuttling,
Fish splashing,
Wind whistling,
Cliffs crumbling,
Seaweed popping,
Dark sky rumbling.

The Farmyard's full of *Noises*

Hens are clucking,
Horses neighing,
Sheep bleating,
Donkeys braying,
Pigs grunting,
Cows mooing,
Ducks quacking,
Ring doves cooing.

The Kitchen's full of *Noises*

Taps are dripping,
Cupboards banging,
Kettle boiling,
Pans clanging,
Chairs scraping,
Cups cracking,
Cutlery clinking,
Plates stacking.

But in the classroom of Mr Hill,
All is silent, all is still.
For all the girls and all the boys
Know that their teacher can't stand noise.
So – **WILL YOU BE QUIET!** Please?

This is the Key

This is the key of the school.
In that school is a classroom,
In that classroom there is a desk,
In that desk there is a drawer,
In that drawer is a box,
In that box are my sweets,
Which Mr Davis confiscated yesterday.

Sweets in the box,
Box in the drawer,
Drawer in the desk,
Desk in the room,
Room in the school.
This is the key to the school.

Decisions! Decisions!

The Kitchen Orchestra

In the kitchen, what a noise!
Listen to those girls and boys,
Banging boxes, clanking pans,
Clacking spoons and tinkling cans.
Tapping bottles, rattling plates,
What a noise the children make!
It sounds just like a band.
Yes, it sounds just like a band.

Bimla bangs the big black box:
Boom, boom, boom-banga-boom.
Kirit clanks the silver pans:
Clank, clank, clank, clank-a-lank.
Colin clacks the wooden spoons:
Clack, clack, clack, clack-a-lack.
Tina tinkles the cans:
Tink, tink, tink, tink-a-link.
Barry taps the empty bottles:
Clink, clink, clink clink-a-link.
Ravjir rattles the round red plates:
Rat-a-tat, rat-a-tat, rat-rat-a-tat.

In the kitchen, what a noise!
Listen to those girls and boys,
Banging boxes, clanking pans,
Clacking spoons and tinkling cans.
Tapping bottles, rattling plates,
What a noise the children make!
It sounds just like a band.

Yes, It sounds just like a band!

The Runaway Train

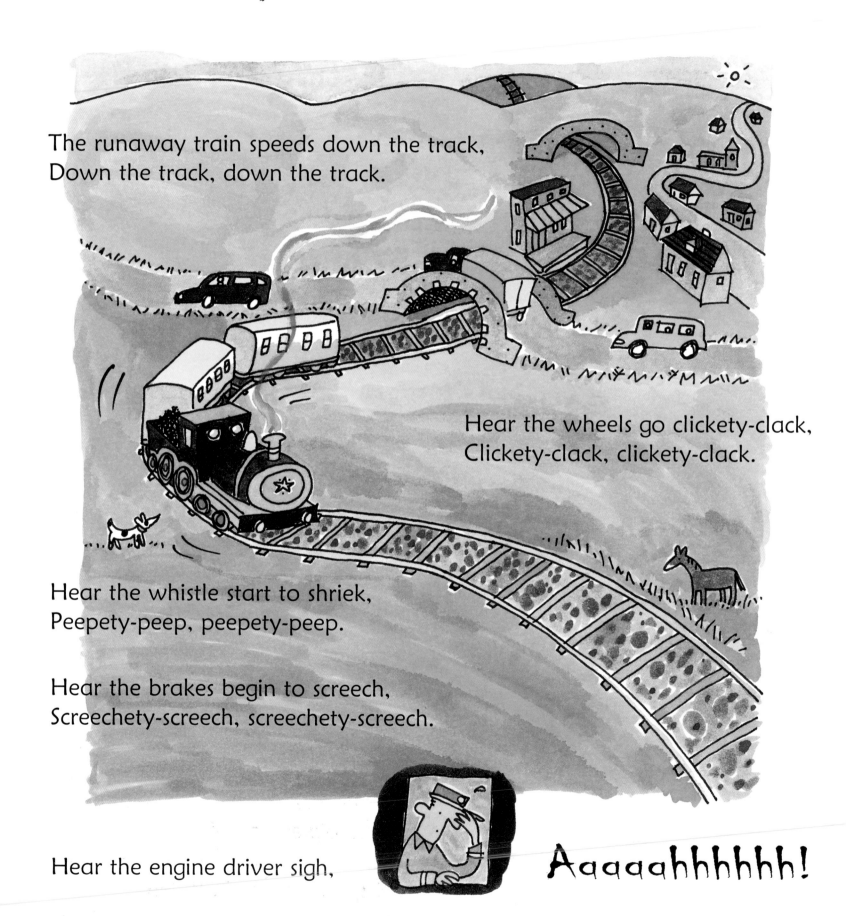

The runaway train speeds down the track,
Down the track, down the track.

Hear the wheels go clickety-clack,
Clickety-clack, clickety-clack.

Hear the whistle start to shriek,
Peepety-peep, peepety-peep.

Hear the brakes begin to screech,
Screechety-screech, screechety-screech.

Hear the engine driver sigh,

Aaaaahhhhhh!

One to Ten

One and two and three and four,
Ten little mice behind the door.
Two and three and four and five,
Fourteen little fishes dive.
Three and four and five and six,
Eighteen squirrels playing tricks,
Four and five and six and seven,
Twenty-two angels up in heaven.
Five and six and seven and eight,
Twenty-six rooks on the garden gate.
Six and seven and eight and nine,
Thirty piglets in a line.
Seven and eight and nine and ten,
Thirty-four foxes in a den.

Five Fat Conkers

Hold fingers downward to represent conkers, leaves, berries, acorns and boy.
Wiggle them as you blow on them, then drop your hand in your lap!

Five fat conkers on the chestnut tree,
Were dangling down for all to see.

Whoosh! came the wind, blowing through the town,
And five fat conkers came tumbling down!

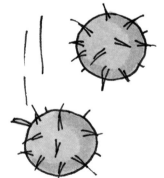

Four green leaves on the sycamore tree,
Were dangling down for all to see.

Whoosh! came the wind, blowing through the town,
And four green leaves came tumbling down!

Three red berries on the rowan tree,
Were dangling down for all to see.

Whoosh! came the wind, blowing through the town,
And three red berries came tumbling down!

Two round acorns on the old oak tree,
Were dangling down for all to see.

Whoosh! came the wind, blowing through the town,
And two round acorns came tumbling down!

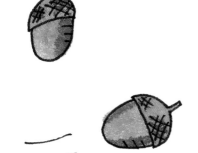

One small boy in the willow tree,
Was dangling down for all to see.

Whoosh! came the wind, blowing through the town,
And one small boy came tumbling down!

What's inside the Apple?

What's inside the apple,
That's firm and round and red?
I thought I saw two tiny eyes,
And a little hairy head.

What's inside the apple,
That's firm and red and round?
I thought I saw a tiny mouth,
And heard a chomping sound.

What's inside the apple,
That's red and round and firm?
Why, I can see a body green,

It's a wiggly, wriggly worm!

My Pet

I don't want a goldfish,
I don't want a cat,
I don't want a gerbil,
A rabbit or a rat.
I don't want a hamster,
A budgie or canary,
I would like a spider,
That's **furry, fat and hairy.**
I'd like to watch him spin his web,
In the early morning light,
And dangle down on his silvery thread,
And tickle me goodnight.

What Creature, Pray, are You?

CRACK, CRACK, CRICKETY CRACK!
The shell had cracked in two.
Snap, Snap, Snipperty, Snap!
What creature, pray, are you?

Are you a little chimpanzee,
Or a baby kangaroo?
An elephant or a tall giraffe?
What creature, pray, are you?

CRACK, CRACK, CRICKETY, CRACK!
The shell had cracked in two.
Snap, Snap, Snipperty, Snap!
What creature, pray, are you?

Are you a little lion cub,
A tiger or gnu?
A cute and cuddly koala bear,
What creature, pray, are you?

CRACK, CRACK, CRICKETY, CRACK!
The shell had cracked in two.
Snap, Snap, Snipperty, Snap!
What creature, pray, are you?

The creature snapped its little jaws,
And smiled a dreadful smile,
"I'm the oldest creature in the world -
I am a crocodile."

CRACK, CRACK, CRICKETY, CRACK!
The shell had cracked in two.
Snap, Snap, Snipperty, Snap!
What creature, pray, are YOU?

The Camel

Do not stare at the camel,
As you are passing by,
For he will turn his dusty head,

And **spit** you in the eye!

The Elephant

The elephant has no fingers,
The elephant has no toes,
But the elephant has enormous ears,

And a very impressive **nose**.

The Yak

If you should meet a hairy yak,
With great sharp horns and a shaggy back,
Just smile and say, "How do you do?"
And he will say the same to you.

Don't stop to pass the time of day,
Just say, "Goodbye" and walk away.
For he can talk from dusk to dawn,
From the evening 'til the early morn.

He'll chatter morning, noon and night,
From sunset to the morning light.
You see, it is a well-known fact,

That yaks, they like to *Yakkety Yak!*

On Old Macdonald's Mixed-up Farm

On Old Macdonald's mixed-up farm
O, I-E, I-E.
Just listen to the noise they make,
And you will soon agree.

The Mouse meows,
The Hen he-haws,
The Dog hoots,
The Duck roars.
The Donkey chirrups,
The Pigeon brays,
The Goat grunts,
The Pig neighs.
The Cat quacks,
The Goose bleats,
The Bull barks,
The Sheep squeaks.
The Cow clucks,
The Lamb coos,
The Horse bellows,
The Turkey moos.

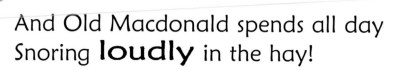

And Old Macdonald spends all day
Snoring **loudly** in the hay!

Humpty Dumpty

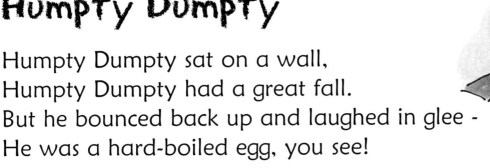

Humpty Dumpty sat on a wall,
Humpty Dumpty had a great fall.
But he bounced back up and laughed in glee -
He was a hard-boiled egg, you see!

Humpty Dumpty

Humpty Dumpty sat on a wall,
Humpty Dumpty had a great fall.
He didn't shout and he didn't scream -
For below him was a trampoline!

Little Miss Muffet

Little Miss Muffet,
Sat on a tuffet,
Eating an ice cream cone.
There came down a **Spider**
Which sat down beside her -
Miss Muffet said, "Leave me alone!"

Little Miranda

Little Miranda,
Sat on the veranda,
Having a noonday nap.
There buzzed down a bee,
Which sat on her knee -
And Miranda said, "Ooh, fancy that!"

Little Miss Mabel

Little Miss Mabel,
Sat at the table,
Eating her curry and rice.
There came down a snake
Which swallowed her plate -
Which really was not very nice.

Oh, What is in that Little Box?

Oh, what is in that little box,
Whatever can it be?

Could it be a spider or a buzzing bumble bee,
A slimy snail or a slippery slug,
Or a tiny jumping flea?

Oh, what is in that little box,
Whatever can it be?

Oh, what is in that little box,
Whatever can it be?

Could it be a wiggly worm,
Wriggling to be free,
A beetle or a spotted bug,
Or a tiny chimpanzee?

Oh, what is in that little box,
Whatever can it be?

Oh, what is in that little box,
Whatever can it be?

I wish that I could open it,
But I haven't got the key.
But wait a mo, the lid is loose,
I'll open it and see.
Oh, look what is in the little box:

The blind mice!

One, Two, Three!

The Grand Old Duke of Kent

Oh, the Grand Old Duke of Kent,
He hadn't any men,
So he marched by himself to the top of the hill,
And he marched right down again.
"It isn't that much fun," he said,
"When you march without an army.
The people who live hereabouts,

They must think that I'm **barmy!**"

Jack and Jill

Jack and Jill climbed up the hill,
Their feet, they felt like lead.
Said Jack, "Oh, let's not bother, Jill,
We'll go to town instead."

To Town →

Mary, Mary, Quite Contrary

"Mary, Mary, quite contrary,
How does your garden grow?"
"I suggest you read a gardening book,
And then you'll get to know!"

What David Draper Dropped

David Draper dropped a dozen delicious donuts.
A dozen delicious donuts David Draper dropped.
If David Draper dropped a dozen delicious donuts,
Where's the dozen delicious donuts David Draper dropped?
Daisy, David Draper's **dribbling** dog, devoured them!
That's what!

Five Little Mice

This little mouse eats chocolate,
This little mouse eats cheese,
This little mouse eats biscuit crumbs,
This little mouse eats peas,
And this little mouse,
He squeaks and squeaks,

"I'll eat just what I please!"

I Would Like

I would like to swing, swing, swing up in the air so high,
I would like to soar, soar, soar like a songbird in the sky.
I would like to dance, dance, dance like a famous ballerina,
I would like to squeeze, squeeze, squeeze like a squeaky concertina.
I would like to dive, dive, dive deep down in the ocean blue,
I would like to jump, jump, jump higher than a kangaroo.
I would like to fly, fly, fly my kite on a windy day,
I would like to slide, slide, slide on Santa's Christmas sleigh.
I would like to swim, swim, swim in a warm and wavy sea,
I would like to climb, climb, climb like a chattering chimpanzee.
I would like to crunch, crunch, crunch through the snow on a winter's day,
I would like to stretch, stretch, stretch in the sunshine in the hay.

But most of all, what I would like,
Is to snuggle up close in my bed at night,
And feel my mum's arms hold me tight,
And cuddle me with all their might.
Yes, that is what I'd really like -

That's what I would really like!